STORMBORN

A TREE OF SILVER NOVELLA

STORMBORN

BETH BALL

ALSO BY BETH BALL

Heir of Lilith

Phantom

Pain

Feather & Flame

Phoenix Rising

Age of Azuria

Buried Heroes

Hadvarian Heist

Amber Queen

Forest Deep

Shadows Beneath

Novellas and Short Stories

Promise, an *Heir of Lilith* novella

Aurora, an *Age of Azuria* novella

Song of Parting, an *Age of Azuria* novella

Story Magic, an *Age of Azuria* novella

Stormborn, a standalone *Tree of Silver* novella

"Blood Wolf Moon", an *Age of Azuria* story

"The Shadow's Embrace", an *Age of Azuria* story

"Nocturne", an *Age of Azuria* story

Published by Grove Guardian Press

Edited by The Blue Garret

Cover design by Mibl Art

Ebook ISBN 978-1-952609-19-0

Paperback ISBN 978-1-952609-20-6

Hardback ISBN 978-1-952609-21-3

groveguardianpress.com

DUR'FOR
HALLOWED HILLS
BASTI
VERITA
THE GLADE OF SHADOWS
T
SCOURGE

NORTHLANDS
FAER HAVEN
VESTIGE
DRAYKEMIRE
MERIDIENNE MOUNTAINS
RESPITE
THE GREEN MOUNTAINS
S-MAEN
THE EMERAUDE
RAL
PALAIS
BEACON
THE WORLD OF ELDURA

CHAPTER ONE

THE DRAGON

For days before the warband's arrival, the acrid scent of woodsmoke and blood drifted toward me. Generations into our conflict, and still the would-be rulers of Draykemire remain unaware of the sharpness of our senses. From miles off, we can hear the pounding of hooves and drumming of feet that announce their presence.

Then why have dragons been driven to the point of extinction, you might ask.

The question is fair, albeit unoriginal.

There's no need for you to be anxious. I am, as yet, unoffended.

Dating back one thousand years, less than a century after the fall of Orison, the Orbaskiers made their foolish vow upon the field of battle. Line upon line of rebel soldiers stood quaking in the face of Erdris's wrath.

It was there she made her last stand, and there, upon that field, that Ilvan Orbaskier swore to the earth below and sky above, to all who could hear—he and his line would not rest until the last dragon of Draykemire had been eliminated. And in our stead, they would rule this land of ours.

Erdris breathed out her curse upon the commander. She, blessed by each of the three fates, condemned her murderers to a life of ill fortune. None would be so unlucky as Ilvan and his offspring.

You are free to shrug at this if you must, but let me assure you, it is no small thing.

For every ill turn there is another. Every opportunity, shimmering gold at a distance, rendered down to ash. The Orbaskiers survived Erdris's curse, but only just. Like ours, their numbers have dwindled. A line that was once many has been reduced to two, and only the faintest trace of their blood flows in the veins of other royals of this land that was once ours.

This land once ruled by dragons.

In making a vow of her own, casting shadow upon the revolutionary and his heirs, Erdris bound their fate to ours. For eternity, our roots intertwine and mingle. The Orbaskiers seek not only our extinction—they wish to drive the very memory of our names from existence.

But we cannot fall, not truly, until they are undone as well.

This much of the story you know, I see. Well enough. Allow me to skip over hundreds of years of turmoil and in-fighting—heir against heir with a smattering of dragon-slaying in between.

We will open instead on that scarlet-glow morning, the day Desdemona Orbaskier led her warband to the foothills of my mountain hideaway. I had assumed that one of the heirs of the Orbaskier line would find me eventually. Of the two remaining heirs, Desdemona seemed far more likely to succeed in such a quest than her cousin Tavian, though he figures in our story as well.

Yes, if you must put it that way, you are right. The day I lost myself and fell in love.

You cannot imagine what a sight she was, seated atop her great black horse as she and her warband crested the hill outside my lair. Desdemona grasped a sword in one hand and bridle in the other. No flash of fear flickered across her face at what she was about to do. No twinge of regret either, I might add.

I had learned to be careful of the two-legged creatures who had overrun our domain, the children of the elves and fae more than the rest. Their keen senses could penetrate the dark of my lair in ways those descended from the Lycan, the humans, had lost.

The wind caught in Desdemona's raven hair, pulling strands across her olive skin. It was a moment I had imagined plenty of times before. When the time came, would I fight or flee? But I had made up my mind already.

My truest chance of survival was to disguise my identity.

Unlike you, lorekeeper, the rulers of Draykemire remain unaware of this special draconic ability.

CHAPTER TWO

DESDEMONA

esdemona raised her fist and called her troops to halt a half-day's ride from what her scouts had reported was the dragon's lair.

Let us see if Tavian can steal this kill from me too. He has taken so much else. But in truth, the fault was her own. It was she who had underestimated the breadth of her cousin's schemes before, in spite of the counsel of her trusted handmaiden Isolde, a seer. The great cowardice that afflicted Tavian, like his father before him, had blinded her from perceiving an underlying drive, an unquenchable desire for power. He had disguised this desire from the people of Draykemire, both his boundless ambition and his unwillingness to involve himself in the advancement of his aims. He hid behind the lines of his father's soldiers, the mages who had served his mother loyally, and asked all of Draykemire to bend the knee and swear their fealty to him and him alone.

He called her a half-breed, as though Orbaskier blood was negated by her mother's fae heritage. The mages had disagreed at first, but when the five most loyal to her disappeared, the others squawked to a different tune.

Tavian was determined to lead. This factored into her every calculation.

But she had bigger plans for Draykemire and its people.

Desdemona was born to lead, and lead she would.

Four years had passed since the mages drove her and her loyalists out of the city, four years of scraping their way through mountain passes, breaking the frozen surface of the rivers in winter for a gulp of water. It did nothing to quench their hunger, but her homeland saw to slaking their thirst.

The court was Tavian's now, with only one way for her to win it back—she'd have to kill the last dragon of Draykemire.

Over the last two months, her scouts had carefully tracked its movements and, from them, deduced the location of its lair. Like Desdemona and her band, the dragon had drifted further and further from the most hospitable regions of Draykemire and into the sparsely populated woodlands of the southern Meridienne peaks. Her stallion stamped his feet—Desdemona and her horse shared an ever-impatient nature and raven-black hair. She smiled and patted his mane. "Only a few hours more."

Ellis, her strongest warrior, strode forward to her side. He bowed at the waist as he would greet a queen. "The scouts have pulled back, my lady. We proceed at your command."

Desdemona looked down her nose at the leader of her soldiers. "We go on foot from here." She winked at Ellis, whose stern expression broke into a tiny grin.

He shouted her command back to the troops as Desdemona dismounted. Tremors of unease rippled toward her from her soldiers. The winter had been hard. Tavian's forces had sniffed out their camp and drove them from their food and supplies. His soldiers torched the provisions, save the wine, rather than turning them over to the hungry village half a hectare away.

But despite this hardship, Desdemona was determined to not allow frostbite or widespread illness and death throughout her camp to break her spirit. Ellis's resolve and Isolde's steadiness had carried her through to the month of the wolf moons.

Her commander would struggle, as would she, when they succeeded in reclaiming her ancestral throne. Though it wasn't true for the others, it was as true for Ellis as it was for her—the wilderness of Draykemire had won them over. It would forever be their home. They would return to the western fort, the one Tavian hadn't found, when the time was right, after they had slain the dragon, while she prepared to reassert her claim. But even the walls of the fort offered a false surety, a confidence she no longer felt owed.

Life is a battle, whether behind walls or beneath the stars. Her ancestors had not conquered this land and driven out the dragons, protected their people, to then shelter in grand palaces while their subjects starved.

Tavian had won the court, but Desdemona had won the true heart of Draykemire. And for that, she would fight on.

E arly morning mist burned off in the rising sun as Desdemona, Ellis, and Isolde picked their way across narrow ledges and climbed over the boulders mounded at the craggy base of the southern Meridiennes. Desdemona kept her short sword close at hand should any predators lurk just out of sight, disguised among the rocks. Legends told of dragons enchanting wolves to protect them—a repetition of the dragon's creator goddess, Rasvana, tricking the great wolf god Fenrir into her service for a year and a day.

Other legends told of dragons who enchanted mortals to their aid. One of her ancestors, in the fiercest years of the fighting between her family line and the dragons, had been so bewitched. The dragons' magic could dull even the heightened wisdom of the fae peoples. After casting the spell and breaking its victim's will, the creature would send their servitors off to do their bidding. Those devoid of their own mind would scout nearby villages the dragons could not easily access or pillage livestock and resources to fill the dragon's belly.

They were capable of a great many other evils, though Desdemona feared their charm more than the rest. Some of the oldest stories claimed that the dragons had once ruled the land of Draykemire, though these seemed too fanciful to be believed.

Her mother had told her the tales of the dragons from infancy, after Tavian's father murdered his brother, Desdemona's father. "The slaughter of dragons is your birthright, Dessie," her mother would say. "Stay true to your ancestor's vow to protect Draykemire from them, and our kingdom will once more be yours."

Desdemona released her mother's words with the mist. Such promises were easily made by ancestors. She would take greater care with her own line and ensure that she did not fill their days with difficulties. If she slayed the last of the dragons now and reclaimed the throne, her offspring would have a chance at following the life they desired. That would be a beneficial legacy indeed.

Several paces ahead of her, Ellis halted. She and Isolde froze as well. The warrior gestured her forward. "We're approaching a cave, my lady," Ellis whispered.

Finally. Her scouts' reports had proven true. "When the passage opens further, allow me to enter first." This was her quest, her destiny. Her prey.

Ellis bowed his head in assent.

Her insistence on leading the way had led to friction between them in their earliest fighting days, but Ellis had since learned to trust her sword as well as his own. Hundreds of years had passed since the Orbaskiers could have afforded to not keep both sharp wits and blades at their sides, if such a time had ever truly graced Draykemire's history and wasn't a faery tale invented by mages tired of discord and strife.

She and Ellis had also learned to rely on the protection of Isolde and her emerald-fletched arrows. The seer perceived what they could not, wherever it hid in the darkness. Oftentimes she sensed its will and plans before even whatever enemy or creature they sought was aware of its own schemes.

There were no others she would rather have by her side as she entered a dragon's lair. And there were none so willing to brave any danger to remain by her side.

The cave bore all the markings of a dragon's den—a dry passageway through the rock, narrow enough to allow curious prey inside but not wide enough to allow multiple outsiders in at once.

"Keep your sword close," Desdemona murmured to Ellis under her breath.

The warrior smirked. He rarely did anything else.

Before her family had made themselves the rulers of Draykemire, when wild dragons still terrorized the populace, the legends about the dragons had attributed all manner of terrifying abilities to the creatures—beasts who could survive in any environment, more cunning than the wisest mage, with golden tongues capable of convincing a shepherd to turn against his lover or a warrior against her liege.

But as they had systematically wiped the scourge from their lands, they had not found impressive hordes of treasure—the dragons coveted prizes far greater than gold.

To the north, her ancestors had discovered a lair filled with herbs and magic plants. Enchanted mortals had tended the underground garden that the dragon had carefully cultivated. Hundreds of rare varieties, many of which their herbalists had never encountered before, kept alive by a false sunlight the dragon conjured with its mind.

The creature had screamed when they set fire to the ceiling, which was lined with drying herbs. The smoke that curled out of the cave was said to have driven the closest village into a collective, three days' long vision.

Those they had freed from the dragon's lair wept to see the creature brought low. Their enchantment ran so deep that they claimed they had served the dragon of their own free will.

In death, the dragon cursed the land, as one of its predecessors had cursed her family line. Within a year of the dragon's demise, the river waters reclaimed the crop-filled fields that had kept the villagers alive. They had no choice but to abandon their homes and travel south, away from the growing marshland.

The witch who had served the village had blamed not the dragon, but its killers, for the destruction of their food source. A great conspiracy of ravens had fallen upon her, croaking over her foul words. She vanished in their midst and was never seen again.

Desdemona rolled away this story-scroll to place in a memory library along with the others as she slid into the entrance of the cave. The library was an imagined apparition, conjured from childhood, before she'd been forced out of Draykemire's capital city, Sanctuary, and the court. Once she had reclaimed the crown and throne, there would be myriad chances to consult the real records, deed after deed of her family line.

There were scant few opportunities to slay dragons and prove her mettle as queen.

If she succeeded, this would be only the second dragon kill of her generation. Her father had found several before he and her mother had met. One of the great conflicts between her father and her uncle had been over the number of dragons each had killed—did a nest full of slathering babes count as one or five? The argument had lasted all their lives, until her uncle had killed her father.

The passageway was narrow. Desdemona turned to the side and slipped one foot around the other to navigate her way forward. The leather pauldrons at her shoulders would protect her neck from a sudden fling of a spear or similar attack, but would not help her if the dragon resorted to its breath-weapon—acid, fire, an enchanted smoke. In that case, neither would her body offer much protection to Ellis or Isolde.

But that was the risk each dragon-hunter took for herself.

CHAPTER THREE
DESDEMONA

An hour's winding path through the tunnels led Desdemona, Ellis, and Isolde into a vast underground cavern. Toothlike stalactites hung dripping from the ceiling. Their roots joined in a vast circle around an opening at the top of the cave, a gaping maw with a throat made of sky—the perfect escape for a monster of legendary proportions.

And at the center of the lair, crouched and rubbing his hands before a fire, was a human man with slicked-back, dark brown hair and gold-rimmed eyes.

Desdemona could not have been more disappointed.

The man kept his head angled down as she approached. Desdemona slid along the sides of the cave, sheltered by the shadows. Ellis emerged close behind her and did the same.

"Are you looking for someone?" the man said to the crackling fire.

Desdemona readjusted the sword hilt in her hand. She could plunge it into the man's gut if he attacked, though she would rather gut him for information about his captor. "For some*thing*, yes."

He straightened from his squatting position, turned toward her voice, and tilted his head to the side. "I'm not sure you'll find it here." The firelight flashed gold in his eyes, a strange trick of the cave.

"Are you here alone?" Desdemona asked. If she could keep the man's attention, Isolde would be better able to study his reactions and see if he had been enchanted by the dragon or not.

He smiled, a bright flare of white.

The warmth of his expression pulled Desdemona toward him. She stepped forward almost without awareness.

Ellis gripped her shoulder. "Wait, my lady."

The man's eyes flickered between them. "I was, but I am no longer." He opened his hands to indicate the three of them.

Desdemona placed her hand atop Ellis's. *I'm alright now.* The excitement of infiltrating the den had clouded her senses. She continued in her sidle along the edge of the cavern, and Ellis did the same in the opposite direction. The three of them had practiced such a maneuver countless times.

The man spared a quick glance for Isolde and Ellis before he pivoted his gaze to follow her. "I have a feeling that these questions are leading somewhere, and as you are the leader of these two, please, be at your leisure and ask away."

Ellis glowered from the opposite side of the cave. The man had erred too closely on the side of issuing her an order for her commander's taste.

Desdemona raised her hand, asking him to wait.

"What you say is true. Answer me this first—What is your name?"

The man rose. He was taller than she'd thought initially, almost as tall as Ellis, though with a slighter build. With a flick of his wrists, he stretched his hands to either side and bowed low from the waist. "You can call me Shar." He clasped his hands loosely in front. The golden light still danced in his eyes. "You hesitate to tell me your name, fair maiden?" His smile broadened. "I am undisturbed by such omissions, and I beg that you will allow me the indulgence of a guess."

Shar wore common clothes and yet spoke as though he was at the center of a prestigious gathering he wished to impress. Not even the vicars and magistrates dared to tempt her with a game or teasing wits. The contrast was surprisingly pleasing.

"Are there terms to this indulgence of yours?" Desdemona asked. It had been years since she had been able to make an anonymous appearance in a town. Was this what others felt like, who walked about without a phantom crown? "A certain prize should you guess correctly, and a boon to me should you fail?"

"The lady sets intriguing terms for one who has wandered into a stranger's cave." He pretended to consider, but the gleam in his eyes remained. "Very well, I undertake your challenge. Should your warrior choose not to gut me"—he glanced over his shoulder; Ellis had indeed stepped closer at Shar's easy banter—"and should I guess true, I would ask but one thing, to place a kiss upon your hand."

Desdemona frowned at the request. There had been many nobles anxious to beget their heirs upon the Orbaskier line, of course, especially those who would swear their fealty to Tavian, kneeling before his feet, but whispering to her in a village alley of the army they would raise to her aid, if she would only take their hand. Shar, however, seemed to genuinely intend the expression of affection and nothing more.

Worse still, Desdemona found herself hoping he would guess right.

She searched the dripping ceiling again for signs of the dragon—had it crept silently into its lair while its next meal distracted them from its arrival? She found only the damp stalactites and their shadowy reflections staring down.

Desdemona allowed herself to smile at Shar's request. She was not often so at ease with strangers. "My squire fell in our most recent battle," she began. Poor lad—he'd been unprepared for the close combat involved for the cavalry. She and Ellis had trained him as best as they were able in a short time, but he had been raised a farmhand and was slow to adjust to the life of a soldier. Such additions did not last in their ranks for long, and yet they insisted upon the chance to join her service. "I need a replacement. Should you fail to guess my name, the position will fall to you."

Hopefully the insult of serving as a squire when he was likely capable of standing in as one of her knights would establish her preeminence and stamp out any confusion his playful manner might bring.

Shar bowed low again. "I accept your terms and hereby stake my vow—Should I fail, I swear my service to you for however long you need."

Desdemona swallowed a sigh. So much for internalizing his position. Shar grew more charmed and charming with each passing moment.

The dragon's captive turned to observe Ellis, who stood with sword lowered yet ready to swing a few paces away. "Your warrior serves close at hand and has protected you for years." He spun back to face her as though Ellis's brawn harbored no threat to him—a perilous miscalculation. "But perhaps the one who still lingers in the shadows performs the more hazardous work—the one blessed to see and work the Weave?"

Isolde's gaze darted toward Desdemona's—she found this cave-dweller engaging as well.

"These clues together, I would guess your name to be Valeria Orbaskier."

Her seer gave a quick gasp of surprise, but Shar's eyes didn't falter from Desdemona's face.

She flexed the fingers of her off-sword hand to release the feelings that fluttered to life at the name. "You are half-correct. I am of the Orbaskier line. Valeria was my mother."

Shar lowered onto his knee and bowed his head in a position of fealty, the move so rapid she could not perceive his expression. "I am sorry for your loss, my lady. Might you be so generous as to allow your lowly squire to know your name in full?"

The deprivations of the brumal season had reduced her numbers so far that she could not hastily turn away proffered aid. And her mother would be honored by such tribute. What harm could there be in such a simple request? "Desdemona."

Shar whispered the name to himself as though it was the most alluring he'd ever heard. Its echo caught across the cave, a cloak draped over her shoulders.

Without allowing herself to mull it over at length, Desdemona strode forward and held her hand out to the kneeling man. "I will take your kiss, for half a name is something though not all, and bid you rise, my squire."

Shar raised his gaze to hers. His irises were the dark blue of a storm-tossed sea and lined with the gold she had perceived upon their first meeting. Gently, he took her hand in his and pressed soft lips against her knuckles.

A small shudder rippled over Desdemona. It curled tighter below her stomach the way tiny dragons nestled in their dens in the storybooks. "Easier to slaughter them that way," her father had supposedly said.

"The terms fall in your favor, Desdemona."

Shar said her name so sweetly, she wanted nothing more than to hear it again. *What is wrong with me?*

She had been too long without companionship, that was all. And she was without the release of a battle with a dragon.

Shar lingered on the cave floor, almost as if he was waiting for her attention to return fully to him. "Your squire I shall be."

⁂

THE DRAGON

Of course I guessed the wrong name—how strange you should ask such a question. I knew one of the remaining Orbaskiers would find me, and the favor was much more on Desdemona's side than her cousin's. She had killed one of my kind already, the youngest in her family to do so.

But knowing who was trespassing into my lair and being prepared to meet my would-be murderer are two different things. Such bewitching dark eyes, an evergreen forest shot through with sprigs of spring green, and lips the dark red of a plum hanging low from a tree. I fell into her thrall immediately.

It was not beauty alone—I wouldn't so diminish your vision of her. The warrior and the fates-witch at her side, they remained captive in her sway as well. Three powerful individuals all trapped in amber by a single elf. Each of her strides bore the signature of a predator, of one accustomed to gaining the upper hand and using it to her advantage.

In truth, lorekeeper, it was all these and none of them that caught me in Desdemona's grasp, never again to be free. She kept a question poised atop her raised brow, a challenge perched on the bow of her lips. From my first whiff of her—dried florals, musk, and damp woodland— winding her way through the tunnels my predecessors had carved, I knew—Desdemona had spent her life searching for her equal. This was comprehension enough, though I did not realize this last until I beheld her—I longed for nothing dearer than for her to choose me as such a match.

CHAPTER FOUR

THE LOREKEEPER

LOREKEEPERS' NOTE

*I*n a time now passed, before Ruka's betrayal sent the city of Orison into the depths of the sea, there was a great and ancient kingdom, Neverune, ruled through the ages with wisdom and might by a sacred line of kings. The kingdom withstood the insistent attacks of Alessandra. The dark goddess was envious of the kingdom's prosperity and longed to overtake the throne for herself. But the line of kings persisted in protecting their city. And their rule lasted for one thousand years.*

But like many a story, such a faery tale could not continue forever.

What the line of kings did not know, in spite of their wisdom and the careful governance of those among them blessed by the fates with sight, was that calamity waited with carefully folded wings. And it chose the perfect moment to strike.

One thousand years after Alessandra's betrayal of the elemental titans, they who carefully governed the workings of the prime plane of Eldura, another mortal rose to the power of godhood.

Ruka, the champion of water, right hand of Thalyssa, betrayed the city he had been appointed to protect. The earth around Orison splintered and burst, sending the city into the gaping maw of the sea. With the sacrifice of thousands of souls, the former champion rose to Alessandra's side.

Ruka ascended from champion to godhood as his mistress had before him. A god of trickery, lies, and deceit, Ruka twisted the minds of Neverune's great kings and turned them against the people they had been appointed to serve. A new line of leaders rose up in their stead, determined to be protectors of the people and to rid the land of the kings' corruption.

War and infighting tore apart the ancient kingdom. Thousands more perished in the fights over who would rule and how.

Distressed by what transpired in their realms and the role their own failures had played, the titans intervened. Thalyssa sent the waters to divide the kingdom, to shrink the influence and power of any single king. Gaia called mountains to rise up from the earth and divide the kingdom still further.

It was not the first time the titans had resorted to separation and rising waters to quell rebellion and bloodshed upon the planes of life, nor would it be the last. From their workings, eventually, peace returned. The city of Respite grew up from the western mountains. To the north, the people created Vestige, a land ravaged by the fallen line of kings who left much of the city in ruins with their fall. The most powerful of the three arose in the east. There, the new line of rebels turned kings continued in their rule. And at the heart of the throne of Draykemire, the dream remains: that one day, the three cities might be united again.

But beneath such an ambition, a truer promise beats on—a benevolent guardian of the people who aims to lead them, who would see the capital city, Sanctuary, restored to the aspiration of its name.

CHAPTER FIVE

THE DRAGON

My first weeks with Desdemona passed in a blur of warriors' faces and moments by her side. One of the only graces that has allowed my kind to survive as long as we have is the fact that our hunters have yet to learn of our ability to transform into bodies similar to theirs. With every breath, I was conscious of the way they moved, of how they spoke to one another. I tried to mimic their mannerisms, to laugh when they did, to make myself appear as one of them.

I have always been fascinated by those most of my own kind rightly consider our oppressors, our exterminators. I cannot help but to feel that there is some reason they loathe us with such ferocious determination, hidden in the half-stories each side tells. Something lingers, lost to the past, that we dragons would rather forget but that an instinctive part of them remembers.

For all our stories of valorous leaders and wise kings, the mortals are right to fear us as they do. Were our numbers greater, I am certain the tides would turn and it would be they who served us rather than the other way around.

Those closest to Desdemona, the warrior named Ellis and the fates-witch, Isolde, watched me with unwavering attention. I knew they would be my greatest threat. And yet in protecting myself from their suspicions, I also found my way to following my own desire—I remained at Desdemona's beck and call and performed whatever task she asked of me. What was more, I allowed the attachment I felt for her, a sense of fates irrevocably intertwined, to linger over my features whenever I was around their lady.

She whom even in my strangest dreams I would never have dared to call mine.

But I was wrong in believing that she did not—could not—care for me, she who had hunted me across the lands her ancestors had passed down to her. My ancestors would have said we were born into these lands and the mortals were nothing more than a pestilence upon them.

All of that changed when Tavian's forces found us that cold morning in early spring.

Desdemona was taking a patrol of her troops and, as her loyal squire, I followed along at her side. I made notes of repairs and munitions as she listed them, of drills for the various groups of soldiers to undertake as the snow melted, of new groupings of combatants to try.

I should have detected some sign of their approach. To this day, I know not how Tavian's scouts eluded even my senses. They were not so lucky the second time, but I digress.

One moment, I stood beside Desdemona as we stared out over the tents and troops that comprised her diminished reign. In the next, poison-covered arrows fell down from the sky.

I reacted as quickly as I was able and pulled Desdemona back from the arrow-fire. I held her against my chest and turned, my body a shield for hers. It was all I could do to not allow my wings to burst forth from my shoulders and cover her in an armored body of scales that would protect her from any chance of harm, but that would have been a death sentence, and my magic reacted even faster than my body.

The winds answered the cry of my heart and blew the second wave of arrows off course. They rained down around us, but they did not strike my lady or myself.

Heedless of her own prowess, I pulled her along to safety, away from the archers' range.

Once clear, I released her. Only a breath-full of seconds had passed.

Thunder cracked overhead, an expression of my distress. For weeks I had tried to keep the storms at bay, and yet here she was before me, under threat and angry, so angry—either at Tavian's assault or my own forwardness, I knew not.

The conflict had heightened my senses. Desdemona stood before me, green eyes ablaze, chest heaving.

And behind her, slithering between the tents just out of sight, was one of Tavian's blades.

I leapt forward and yanked Desdemona's sword from her side. Two strides more and a single swing behind was all I needed—I swiped the soldier's head free from his neck, and he and his poisoned dagger fell to seep their foul fluids onto the earth.

With care, avoiding my lady's eyes, I wiped the blade clean. I knelt and offered it back to her as more lightning and thunder crackled overhead.

She seized the sword's grip with such surety and charge.

The first raindrops fell from the sky.

Desdemona raised an eyebrow as she stared down at me. "Well then, you've certainly proven your steadfastness."

I could not help my answer, nor would I take it back even now, after everything. "My lady," I said, "I would prove that and so much more."

The corners of her eyes narrowed—whether she took my meaning or not, I couldn't tell. My courage failed me in that moment of confusion, and I rose without her permission, spun about, and pulled the sword from the assassin's side. "There will be more of them about," I told her. "Keep a sharp eye."

I strode away then, my senses aware of every pattering strike of the rain. I knew the faces, the hair and shoulders of Desdemona's ranks. And I knew the forms of those who slunk between their tents and those who gathered outside their lines.

The archers I dealt with easily enough. Most I slew with lightning strikes. To the untrained observer, it would have looked like an accidental stretch of luck but was in fact something far worse. The rest fled back to their master.

I hunted the spies with delight. A spark had kindled within me the moment I held Desdemona in my arms.

Weeks ago, I would have let the Orbaskiers continue their in-fighting over lands that, as dragons tell, had only recently become theirs, in our draconic rather than mortal terms.

But after, I wanted what she did, the future her ancestors had chosen for her themselves.

I wanted Tavian dead.

In the meantime, I settled for any who swore their fealty to him and who would harm my lady and her servitors.

&a,

DESDEMONA

Desdemona's hands shook as she peeled off her bracers and tossed them to the floor of her tent. Wind battered the white silk of the tent sides.

Tavian's forces had come close. Too close. If Shar hadn't been standing where he was, hadn't reacted so quickly—

Free of her armor, she stumbled over to the turquoise bowl of water at her bedside. Droplets splattered across the thick rugs underfoot as she raised a splash of water to her face. Her hands came away orange-red with watery blood.

She pressed her hands against her leather-covered thighs and looked at her reflection in the mirror.

The heavy shades of dark purple powder around her eyes had smudged in the fighting that ensued as they chased down Tavian's archers. In her travels, she'd heard stories of leaders and knights who had honored the retreat of their opponents and allowed them to return to the safety of the enemy's lines.

Desdemona had scoffed at this. When no scouts returned, that sent a stronger message.

Tavian had not sent many. He had all of Draykemire at his disposal. The purpose of this attack was to test her defenses and rattle her troops. Her rival was simply biding his time and waiting for a more opportune time to attack.

When he did, would they be ready?

Instead of strategy or a counterattack, all she could think about was the way Shar's hands had gripped her waist and pulled her back from the first volley of arrows. How closely he had held her as he put himself between her and the poisoned death raining down from the sky.

"Are you alright?" he had asked, both of them breathless. He had pushed her hair back from her face and stared into her eyes. The deep sapphire rimmed in gold pulled her in deeper.

She only nodded, not yet able to speak.

Shar's face had changed, twisted, and her heart had faltered in the center of her chest. He bellowed and pulled the sword from her hip. In a single swipe, he felled the assassin who had snuck his way into their camp to kill her.

Before she could react, Shar had reached down and taken the assassin's blade for his own. He bowed to her and held out her sword—"Apologies, my lady"—and he sprinted away to defend the lateral front. Ellis was quick to join by his side.

The rest of the afternoon's fighting blurred behind her eyes. Her muscles twitched in memory of the movements they'd perfected, hard-won over years and years of training, first for practice, then necessity.

Why would this other realm be opening before her now? If she ever hoped to secure the throne for herself, as was her right, her duty, and her oath, she had to remain focused on that aim and that alone. She who was so accustomed to the fight, was she to be undone by a swell of feeling for one sworn to her service? A feeling she couldn't hope that he might reciprocate. It wasn't as though he had joined willingly. Her company was preferable to life as a dragon's meal, nothing more. And yet—

Beyond the dripping image of her face and the smear of crushed amethyst beneath her eyes, Shar appeared, the tent opening flapping in the wind behind him. His tattered garments matched the state of her reflection—torn sleeves, blood from different bodies and his own mingled across his person.

He rushed toward her, and Desdemona turned.

His arms wrapped around her again, and he held her tight to his chest.

Desdemona found his lips with hers and pressed her hips closer. Shar kissed her back. She tugged her arm free and caught the back of his head in her hand, holding him near.

This was what she had needed, what she had been waiting for.

The camp and her soldiers would hold for a few hours.

They each had their own way of celebrating that they had survived.

Desdemona wanted a new sort of celebration. One that truly embraced being alive.

She angled Shar back toward her pile of pillows and the bedroll in the back corner of her tent.

Breathless minutes passed, and Shar rolled her weight from atop his hips to underneath him. He stared down at her. Pain and longing flickered behind his eyes. "I was worried something would happen to you."

Desdemona smirked. She wasn't ready yet for such a serious turn, not when the drums of battle had taken up such an intriguing new beat through her bloodstream. "They'll come back in force before long."

Shar smiled at her and shook his head. "But not tonight."

"Hmm." Desdemona grinned back. "No, not tonight."

Her squire pinned her hands to the bedroll and lowered his lips toward her ear. "Then we should make the most of the time that we have."

Skin against skin, they passed the evening in moans muffled against necks and searching hands, the other never more than half a reach away. But one moment, more than all the others, remained with Desdemona long after their love-making was over and a new chapter of their story had begun—Shar cupped his hand beneath her chin and rubbed her cheek with his thumb as though he too couldn't quite believe she was there in his arms.

An object of beauty, of passion, of ferocious strength, she had been all of these before, but never one of sheer wonder. That moment would always and never be enough, but in spite of this, the way he gazed at her said what words could not adequately express. And Desdemona met his adoration in kind.

The prickle of Shar's beard awoke Desdemona the next morning as he whispered in her ear, "Fairest, your other servitors grow anxious of your well-being."

Desdemona groaned and shook her head. Of course they did. "If Isolde and Ellis would be less secretive about their own affairs, they would be passing a far pleasanter morning than flitting about waiting for me to emerge."

Shar chuckled, the low rumble of a distant waterfall caught against the nape of her neck. Her stomach fluttered. "Shall I tell them that their lady is well and satisfied and in need of nothing more than a few hours' additional rest?" As he spoke, his hand trailed over her waist to the base of her ribs and up the swell of her breasts. Shar pinched her nipples to accent his question and chuckled again at Desdemona's gasp.

She was sore from his ministrations during the night, but still—

Desdemona angled her hips back toward his and grinned at her lover's sharp intake of breath as she pressed her backside against him.

Faster than she could believe, Shar's hand shot down to her hips and held her there. "Or," he murmured, his breath hot against her nape, "will my lady need the entirety of the morning to assess certain strategies?"

His fingertips grazed over the line of her hip bone and meandered across her pelvis between her thighs. Shar hummed with satisfaction as she relaxed against him. He traced a circle in time with her quickening breath and murmured a lover's encouraging commands as he brought her nearer to climax.

Desdemona's eyes rolled back, but she seized his hand just before he could send her over the edge again. She swung her legs over his hips and held his hand tight in hers. "So obsequious this morning."

Shar's smile was bright as the sun's insistent rays against the sides of her tent. "I wish only to pay my lady the fealty and respect she deserves."

"Is that so?" Desdemona raised an eyebrow. "It is only fair for a future queen to honor such a reasonable request."

So she did.

CHAPTER SIX

THE LOREKEEPER

LOREKEEPERS' NOTE

*A*s *with any other species, dragons are not all one and the same, whatever the Orbaskier line of Draykemire might claim. They have been more beset upon than most, in part due to the ravages of time, in other cases due to blood feuds like those that began in Draykemire. And while preservation is one of the key tenets of our oaths, the survival of each species was not part of the original purview of our efforts.*

But as the fates will and the Weave dictates, even we must change.

It is not in the interest of our order to mediate the disputes between dragons and the kingdoms that time has spread across their ancestral lands. However, it is in our interest to protect our world from the imbalances of power that have brought about destruction, even outright war, in the past.

We are a created, curated collective of record-keepers. The dragons are lore cultivators by nature. This makes us something akin to allies, in most cases, if not outright friends.

After the loss of certain key locations and the dissolution of several of our most promising alliances, our strategies shifted along with our loyalties. The founder of our order worked at length to befriend one of the dragons and gain his trust. In exchange, she promised to ensure the survival of his kind as best as she was able, though at the time, they both knew what a difficult promise that would be to keep.

In order for her to make such a promise, she had to know the dragons' numbers, kinds, and abilities, for how else could she endeavor to protect them and allow them to survive?

These records have proven most fruitful as new dangers come to light.

The dragons are indeed more closely tied to the magic of Verdigris than certain subsets of legend would have us believe. Their bond to the goddess Cassandra allows them access to the magic that moves between the planes, much like the saudad. They also bear the charms of their creatrix, Rasvana, and many possess the magical command of one or multiple elements, as the druids do.

What is most fascinating to researchers such as ourselves, however, is also one of our best-kept secrets—there exist dragons capable of changing their form and adapting the body and mannerisms of any of the two-legged races who roam these lands. This mutation, so far as we can tell, appears to be a more recent alteration to their magical signatures, though perhaps we have no record of previous instances of shape-shifting because there was no need.

Regardless, this ability to disguise their form and appear as a mortal is one of the dragons' best chances at survival. Though, as always, such surprises and trickery may also spell certain doom.

Our leader was uncertain at first whether she should keep such a development to herself, but she and her dragon ally agreed —there was every chance that sooner or later, the mortal peoples of our world would discover the dragons' secret. Whenever this occurs, there will be panic and blame and the carnage that so often accompanies that pair.

The dragons' best chance of survival is for the mortals to have no idea of such a possibility. We have kept their secret, and had planned to keep it for all time.

But our dragon ally's account to our keepers made note of a concerning anomaly—There is one dragon who has disappeared from our records and ranks. A fire-breather. Like our confidante, he has adapted the ability to shift his form and take on that of a mortal, most often appearing as a half-elf with white hair.

Our ally confided this in part due to his own concerns that such a powerful individual of his species might wander free. He more than most retains the power-lust of his ancestors, the conviction of the dragons' superiority over any rank and class of species, and the desire for domination that these two entail.

We have continued to search for him for over three hundred years, yet our tireless efforts have been to no avail.

It is the conviction of our leader—of all our ranks—that when this dragon presents himself again, he will endanger the close-kept secret of himself and the others, and though he vows revenge upon his hunters, he will bring about the destruction of the dragons instead.

CHAPTER SEVEN
DESDEMONA

As the snows melted, Desdemona and her soldiers carved out a fort in the southern mountains, a spring camp safe from the patrols of Tavian's scouts. Their hidden camp to the northwest remained a possible place for retreat, but they needed somewhere nearer at hand to recover from the harsh winter and sudden ambush.

During this time of rebuilding, Shar remained almost constantly by her side. She spent the afternoons with Ellis and Isolde, planning their return to the northern side of the mountains, a surprise attack against Tavian's troops come fall.

Desdemona sent out riders to the mountain villages with assurances that their future queen yet lived and a new era would be soon at hand.

But in spite of her shielded location, the conviction of her guards, and Isolde's careful enchantments, Tavian's troops found them anyway.

They attacked with fire in the middle of the night. Desdemona awoke to screams and a cold bedroll beside her. She tugged her sword from its scabbard and sprinted outside.

"Shar!" she cried as she slid free of the silk tent flap.

Flames roared from the outer edges of her camp. A ball of fire, impossibly sized, wheeled through the air, slowly turning over itself before it crashed down along the lines of combat. Warriors on both sides screamed as their bodies became flares against the night.

Desdemona gasped and stumbled back. No, there was no other way forward. She strode on, armorless, with only her sword to protect her.

Tavian's scouts must have slaughtered her guard and broken through their advanced defenses in the night.

Desdemona rolled her shoulders back and sprinted toward the front lines. As she ran, she shouted to wake her sleeping ranks. The space outside their camp swelled with hundreds of soldiers, each battalion marked by torches.

How had so many arrived through the winding hills without warning? Some foul magic was on Tavian's side.

His firemancers struck again. They rained fiery death upon her camp without compunction. So long as her soldiers fell, they cared not who else they destroyed.

What she wouldn't give for a smattering of rain to quench the flames.

And almost as soon as she wished it, a boom of thunder in the sky promised to comply.

Soldiers stumbled out of their tents at her cries. One bowed, seeing her there before him.

As he rose, his eyes widened. His mouth gaped open.

Brilliant orange lit his face.

The heat caught against Desdemona's hair.

She threw herself to the side just before the blast.

The soldier and his tent exploded in burning shrapnel.

Desdemona rolled onto her side. They'd set the camp into the craggy hill. She had a perfect view of the slaughter along her front lines below.

A half-elf with hair the color of moonlight stood tall in the center of Tavian's ranks. He swirled his hands together in front of his waist, and a ball of fire grew.

"No!" Desdemona screamed from her perch near the top of the camp.

The mage smiled. The flames reflected on his face, a gold and red glow.

He released the ball of fire as one would a bird, with a whisper and slight flick of his fingers.

The flames struck her ranks. They wiped out more than a dozen of her soldiers and their opponents.

Only smoldering ash remained.

Tavian's forces bellowed in victory at the sight, though many of their own had fallen. They surged into a gap in her lines.

Ellis urged her soldiers forward. He darted into the space between them himself and felled three of Tavian's fighters in one swipe of his sword.

The firemancer narrowed his eyes. He began his incantation again.

Isolde will know what to do. She could search for Shar after the fighting. He had proven himself more than capable the last time.

For now, she had to continue on. The seer would call upon some secret magic to save them, to rescue their ranks. Desdemona pushed herself up. Her stomach rolled as she saw again the reverence twist to panic on the soldier's face before the firemancer's blast consumed him.

Desdemona shouted for Isolde rather than her lover.

She had a responsibility to those that fought for her, a duty she had to uphold.

Questions darted as snakes at her flying heels as she ran through the camp, searching for the seer. Why would Shar have disappeared on the eve of such an attack instead of staying to fight by her side?

Because he betrayed you, a cruel whisper—the voice of one of her ancestors—taunted in the back of her mind.

A flurry of verdant sparks flared ahead to Desdemona's right. Isolde glanced back at her, eyes as green as the magic she cast. Desdemona paused to catch her breath.

Three of her shield-bearers fought at Isolde's side. They struck back at arrows and protected her mage from incoming attacks as Isolde slipped further inside herself and worked the Weave of the field of battle from afar.

Isolde brought her hands together and whispered into the dark pool that grew between her palms.

Purple smoke swirled around the feet of Tavian's forces. Undulating shadows traipsed toward the firemancer in the night.

Her seer already knew what needed to be done. Desdemona nodded to the soldiers who performed their roles as well. She was the one out of place.

She'd been out of place since the dragon's den.

This was a fight for her throne.

The firemancer cast glittering sparks at the phantoms Isolde conjured and sent to surround him. Overhead, the clouds darkened and grew.

Desdemona raised her sword and charged toward the front lines.

Her soldiers needed to see her there, fighting for them. Fighting for the Draykemire they had never seen, but the hope they knew.

She fended off a pair of assassins who crawled through the night. The dark green of Tavian's poisoners dripped from their blades. Their blood stained the tents and seeped into the earth.

So much death, all around her.

This was all she had known.

The press grew closer as Desdemona fought her way to the front. Her soldiers rallied as their queen appeared.

A dark silhouette burst out of the fire-ridden night and landed in a warrior's stance at her side. "My lady." Ellis bowed his head over his sword. He pulled her back and away from the front lines. "There is something I must tell you, that I witnessed this night."

"It can wait till the end of battle or the dawn." Desdemona started back toward the close clumps of her soldiers.

Her warrior caught her wrist. "Please—" His brow furrowed as though he knew the pain his words would inflict. "Please, my lady, you must not. There is a danger closer still. Shar, he—"

Desdemona stopped. "Where did he go?"

Ellis set his jaw and looked toward the heavens.

He's dead.

Again her stomach rolled. She placed her hand against her throat to quell the bile.

"No," Ellis said, "we were mistaken before. He's—"

The din of battle fell away and the cries of soldiers rent the air. One voice rose above the rest. "DRAGON!" the warrior screamed.

Ellis dove and caught his arms around her shoulders. He pinned Desdemona to the ground.

Of course the beasts would find them at such a time. The ill-fortune of the Orbaskiers had never found such an appropriate expression.

Desdemona wriggled out from Ellis's hold. They searched the skies for the dragon's next site of attack. "We should have waited in that dragon's lair and killed it," she scolded herself.

"No, my lady," Ellis answered. "You must understand—"

Thunder boomed so loudly overhead it resounded over Ellis's voice and rumbled through her chest.

She shook her head to clear her senses. What was Ellis trying to tell her? Had Shar been eaten by the dragon?

"Must understand what?" she shouted over the ringing in her ears.

The dragon swept low over Tavian's lines. Thunder roared overhead, and bolts of lightning struck back at their enemy's troops.

Tavian's soldiers shrieked and sprinted away.

The dragon flew low again. It scooped up three infantry soldiers in its shining maw, flew high, and dropped them down as flailing boulders upon their own lines.

The firemancer shifted in his attacks. Tavian's ranks tightened their circle around him. He raised both hands overhead and pelted the dragon with streams of fire.

The dragon dove down toward the firemancer. It lashed at him and the ranks encircled around him with its tail and its teeth. And though the encircled knights fell, the firemancer stood firm.

The soldiers clumped toward the center pushed the corpses away. Others darted close to fill any gaps in their ranks.

As they watched, Ellis repeated, "It's Shar—"

"I cannot worry about Shar right now," Desdemona snapped. Why did she continue to allow the squire to muddle her mind? She had far more pressing concerns than the fate of her vanished lover. The dragon seeming to come to their defense was puzzling enough. Had Tavian and his soldiers tracked down the same lair where they'd discovered Shar? Perhaps the creature had blamed her cousin's troops for stealing its bait—a fine twist of fate indeed. Desdemona laid her hand on Ellis's arm. "We must take advantage of the dragon's inexplicable aid and regroup," she urged. "While the dragon is busy with them, ready our forces. We'll mount a counterattack."

Ellis shook his head. "No, my lady. We cannot. Our numbers were so weakened by the surprise—"

"Do as I command," Desdemona ordered. Her eyes flashed, almost in time to the streak of lightning overhead.

Her warrior bowed his head and obeyed. Ellis sprinted away and returned to the front lines, calling the cavalry to their mounts. The mountain horses of Draykemire had been trained to charge in the face of fear, whether dragon or enemy's might.

Desdemona surveyed her troops as Ellis led the counterattack. Halfway between where she stood and the mountain's peak, Isolde's magic glowed, amethyst and jade in the dark of the night.

The hearts of her soldiers could hold an hour more. They would wipe away Tavian's numbers before the sun rose.

Ellis and the other riders would need aerial support, especially if the dragon's attention turned.

Desdemona called the archers to her side. They climbed over the piled boulders, past the bloodied corpses of friend and foe.

Against all odds, the firemancer drove the dragon back. Almost as soon as she and her archers prepared their shots, the creature reared away and flew away back toward her lines.

"At my signal!" Desdemona cried.

She waved her sword overhead and ducked low.

A volley of glimmering arrows burst forth behind her.

The dragon's cry pierced the sky. It flapped out of the way, flying too high for them to reach without endangering their own lines.

"Take cover," she shouted.

The archers dove from their perch atop the hill. They sheltered among the boulders and watched the dragon's flight.

It screeched again. Powerful wings beat down with the sound of rolling thunder.

She had prepared to face this dragon already. She wouldn't allow a second opportunity to pass her by.

Desdemona ground her teeth and sprinted up the ash-ridden hillside. The skeletal remains of her troops, murdered by Tavian's firemancer, shone in the moonlight.

I will fly, I will not flee. Your death will secure my crown.

The dragon would feel her rage at taking Shar, at devouring him as it had planned to do all along.

"Dragon!" she called in the old tongue, the one the mortals and dragons once shared, "I've no fear of thee!" Desdemona brandished her sword and prepared for her strike as she ran.

The dragon's head skimmed low along the ground. The winds battered her as she sprinted closer.

But she was swift. She would have the chance for one blow before it seized her.

Desdemona swung at the bark-covered scales of its golden neck. The dragon dodged just in time. It reared away and roared at the sky. Bolts of lightning darted out from the center of its shining mouth.

She pushed herself back up to her feet from where she'd rolled away, and the dragon's head swung low again. Sapphire eyes rimmed in gold stared back at her.

Desdemona's breath caught.

No. It cannot be.

The low-hanging smoke was clouding her eyes, that was all. She raised her sword and charged forward again.

The dragon was waiting, head lowered.

Gold flashed in his piercing gaze.

Desdemona sobbed out the hope she had held, that had carried her through the battle this far. She would know him anywhere.

Her knees shook beneath her and she lowered her sword to her side. "Shar," she whispered. It couldn't be true, such things could not be.

The dragon raised its head, and its call rent the sky. Its neck glowed, the metallic shades of a grove of birches caught in the sun's first light.

Desdemona stumbled back and brought her hands to cover her ears from the throbbing call. Time slowed as the dragon looked down at her again. Its head tilted to the side, studying her. "No," she cried. "You were—we—"

A deep voice, both familiar and strange, spoke inside her mind. *The day we met, you asked me my name. I declare it to you now in full, mortal queen—Sharr'kahn,*" the dragon sighed in a voice of thunder and smoke. His wings beat against the air.

Desdemona shielded her eyes but didn't look away from her lover, shifted into his true form. "Why didn't you tell me?" she screamed at the beast.

"This you already know."

Her warriors called out from behind her and sprinted nearer.

The dragon screeched at them again, and they fell back. *"Fare thee well, Orbaskier daughter,"* Sharr'kahn said inside her mind. *"May you find the fate you seek in time."*

Her thoughts would not clarify. Such a transformation, it wasn't possible. Desdemona fell to her knees.

Arrows pelted her lover. They tinged off the armored bark of his scales. Desdemona shouted at her archers to stop, but a roll of thunder drowned out her voice.

Lightning flashed from cloud to cloud, and Sharr'kahn took to the sky.

Strong hands seized Desdemona's shoulders and pulled her back to the safety of her lines. "Thank the goddess you're alright," the soldier said.

Desdemona stared blankly at the kind, rounded eyes that met hers. Never again would she gaze upon adoring orbs of sapphire and gold.

A dragon . . .

She shut her eyes and still the dragon's gaze pierced through her defenses. The spirits of her ancestors struggled against their bonds. They called down from the branches of the trees. *You know that voice of thunder and smoke, unworthy heir. Your bones will find no rest beneath the tree.*

Such punishment she deserved, though it was they who had called the wretched fate and ill-fortune upon themselves and their descendants. It would have been better if she had spared all those around her from the taint of her family's curse.

Those closest to her—

Desdemona's breath caught again. She pushed through

the gathered archers to see through the smoke to the front.

Tavian's forces had retreated. Sharr'kahn didn't pursue them. He flew away, a black silhouette, an absence of stars.

Her cavalry thundered after Tavian's fleeing troops.

A single glow of orange blossomed in the center of their ranks.

Desdemona screamed a warning, but she was too far away.

The front line of her horses burst into flames.

D esdemona clambered down the mountainside. Her mind drifted about, high above.

Body upon body, her soldiers lay slumped. She sprinted across the blood-soaked field. The burning ribs of horses impaled the bodies of their riders.

Ellis had been first in the line of the riders, always ready to lead, and she found him at the front.

Death gripped him in its ashen grasp.

The death she had sent him to.

Desdemona collapsed beside the still form of her warrior. She gagged on her cries as she laid her hand against the deep gash at his side and braced the other behind his neck. "Ellis . . ."

Burning tears streamed from her eyes and mingled with the soot on her face.

Ellis's eyelids fluttered. "My lady—"

"I'm here." Desdemona pulled the cloak from her back. The perfume of blood and flame washed over the two of them. She balled the heavy velvet together and pressed it against the wound at his side.

So much of him was missing. Blood where flesh and bone should be.

"I failed you," Ellis sighed. His breath gurgled. The firemancer's blast had punctured his lung.

"*Shh,*" Desdemona soothed. "You have done no such thing." She searched the smoldering battlefield for Isolde.

"Your dragon," Ellis whispered, "he is gone."

Desdemona shook her head. What she'd seen couldn't be true. It wasn't possible.

The dragon had taken Shar, devoured him, or renewed his enchantment. She couldn't have given herself over to—

Ellis took her hand in his. His grasp was steady, hers shaking. "Tend to the others, my lady. It is too late for me."

"No." Desdemona renewed her efforts to stop the bleeding, but even near death, Ellis held firm. She sobbed again. "I can't do this without you. I never imagined—"

"But you must." The warrior smiled and shut his eyes. He took another slow, rattling breath. "Tell Isolde of my love. I will wait for her in Astralei." Ellis sighed. "She will take care of you both, between now and then."

Both? "Ellis, who are you speaking of?"

He didn't answer.

Desdemona raised up taller on her knees. Her tears fell upon the warrior's face as she rubbed the stubbled line of his jaw. "Ellis?" She grasped his shoulder and shouted his name.

His eyelids and chest were still.

Desdemona fell back upon her heels and screamed at the heavens. Her cry broke off as her voice gave out, her throat rubbed raw by the smoke. She crumpled over the body of her most loyal soldier, her friend.

Isolde would never forgive her.

"Ellis, I'm sorry," Desdemona sobbed. This was her

fault. If she had not been blinded by her infatuation, if she had paid closer attention to the threats swarming all around her rather than the distraction of her heart—

Her stomach rolled, and Desdemona twisted on her knees in the fire-churned earth. The retching curled her spine, bent her back.

"My lady!" Isolde cried as she limped to Desdemona's side. One of the soldiers helped her, but Isolde pushed him away. "My lady . . ." Isolde said again. She clasped a glass vial in her hand.

The seer's face paled in the ashen light. Her gaze stretched beyond Desdemona to Ellis's body, flat and covered in blood. Her hand slackened, and the elixir fell onto the rocky soil. It shattered in an amethyst cloud at Isolde's feet, and she crumpled into a ball, her face lost in her skirt.

"Isolde . . ." Desdemona's voice broke again. She crawled toward her seer.

Isolde's shoulders shook, and she wrapped her arms tighter around her knees.

She called for Isolde once more, begging her to look up. Desdemona reached Isolde's feet and tugged at her gown. "Isolde, please—"

The seer's head shot up from her lap. Hatred flared behind her gaze. "You and your family have taken every-thing from me." Anger coated Isolde's voice in tones Desdemona had never heard.

Alto chanting undergirded the seer's speech, as though Isolde spoke as three beings and not one. "Curse your line and curse your child, Desdemona Orbaskier. Your family's doom you cannot outrun. Bound to the dragons you hunt you were, are, and always shall be. There is no escape from your curse, no limit to your suffering." Isolde's eyes glowed bright purple. "The curse shall be your end. And it will end us all."

Desdemona darted away from the seer as though she'd been burned. Instinctively, her hand clasped the base of her stomach.

Isolde sat frozen. She stared toward Ellis's body.

Finally, the rains broke free. The smoke-laden wind changed, and the anger drifted free from Isolde's face. It left behind only pain.

The seer exhaled. She tilted her head as she beheld Desdemona and her fear. "My lady—" Isolde looked past her again, and her lip trembled. "My love." Tears marred the covering of soot on her cheeks.

Desdemona turned to stare at the hand placed over her stomach. First Ellis, and then Isolde—on an evening of tragic impossibilities. The child of an elf and a dragon . . . Of a mother cursed to ill fortune, who brought all around her to doom.

"His last words were of his love for you," Desdemona said around the knot in her throat.

Isolde bowed her head, the sight's possessive hold passed. "He waits for me in Astralei," she answered, half-song, half-prayer. Isolde raised her gaze to Desdemona's. "Twenty years after the birth, I will join him there."

CHAPTER EIGHT

DESDEMONA

A frigid rain fell as they lit the dawn pyre for Ellis and the others who had fallen. Though spring-melt trickled across the steep hillside of their camp, the cold grasp of winter held the heart of Desdemona's ranks. She clutched frozen fingers against the damp leather of her jacket. Raindrops fell in tiny rivulets down her face, across paths already carved by tears.

She deserved the sideways looks from her soldiers, the whispers that broke off at her approach. If she had acted with more wisdom, if she hadn't allowed herself the distraction with Shar, Ellis would still be beside her now.

Her hopes for the throne had never looked so bleak. More than half her soldiers had perished in Tavian's attack, and still the firemancer roamed free.

Desdemona knew what her soldiers were saying about her across the camp—that Shar had abandoned her at the first chance he got, or that he had been a spy for Tavian's forces all along. Others, that he had fallen to the dragon's maw with no trace left.

The truth rattled her far more.

She had given her heart to the enemy of her family, her people. All Shar's curious questions about herself and her line, were they nothing more than espionage for the dragon Sharr'kahn?

No, whatever she wanted to believe, that wasn't true.

Desdemona placed her hand low on her abdomen, where her child, her child with a dragon, slowly grew.

Ellis had known, before the end, yet he didn't despise her. He had tried to help them, had promised the aid of Isolde to her and the child both.

Isolde who would wear black for the rest of her days because of Desdemona's poor leadership.

Isolde whose shoulders shook beside her, whose bed would remain cold without Ellis to sneak into it when they thought no one knew.

She had failed them all.

"My lady," Isolde whispered.

Desdemona raised her head.

The entire assembly who gathered around the pyres watched her.

Fewer than one hundred souls who trusted her to lead, who had believed in her claim to the throne.

"It is customary for you to speak," her seer murmured. "Please, you must."

Desdemona shuddered and nodded to her friend, the one she had failed.

She drew a cold, wet breath through her nose and pulled her shoulders back. With a few long strides, she brought herself before her lines and raised her head to speak.

The flames of Ellis's pyre warmed her back and dried her hair. If she closed her eyes, the phantom of her warrior friend was there.

"With so many pyres burning, I cannot help but to say that I have fallen short in my service, my guidance, of you all," Desdemona began.

Hollow, desperate eyes stared back at her, confirmed the nagging whispers of the voices deep inside.

"The press of Tavian's attacks grows more dire, and our numbers dwindle." Another sniffle of cold. Desdemona pushed a wet clump of hair back behind her ear. "I speak to you this day not as one who would be your queen, but as one who has bled and fought by your side. As one who has lost friends—" Her voice broke, and she gestured back toward Ellis's body behind her. "And more than friends."

Her hand returned protectively to her stomach. Would Shar embrace her and their child in such a way if he knew? Or would he have left her regardless?

"I speak to you as a fellow warrior and friend, as one who finds herself, like you, standing before a crossroads."

Desdemona stared back at the marred faces of her soldiers. Most were streaked with blood and soot from the battle and the pyres. They each held the losses dear.

Had her father made a speech like this when the strength of his rebellion faltered? Before her uncle's traitorous blade had found its way between his ribs and his strength had failed?

Perhaps it didn't matter anymore.

Before she met Shar, had she ever given herself the chance at a different life? A different future? And for her warriors, who would choose a different path for them?

Desdemona raised her voice. "We must choose this day which Draykemire we will fight for, which version of ourselves we will nurture, strengthen, and seek to grow."

Though the brows of her troops remained furrowed,

the energy around her shifted. The rain pelted down, but they stood firm.

"Do we serve a Draykemire ruled by a despot and his court, one that exists for the furthering of a single line?" She spoke faster. The drums of war returned to her blood. "Or do we serve a Draykemire where the rank of one's birth matters not? Do we fight for a world where all have the right to choose?"

A smattering of soldiers nodded. A few whooped and clapped.

Desdemona smiled. "There is much I have gotten wrong in our time together, my friends. I will not lie to you and pretend otherwise. Some whom we have believed allies proved themselves to be otherwise." She glanced at Isolde. "While some we first found as friends proved themselves to be much more."

Isolde nodded to her. Her forgiveness settled with cold wings upon Desdemona's heart.

"But if the child growing within me is any indication" —a collective gasp flitted across the lines of her troops— "then we still have much to accomplish, much to hope for and to do.

"At this crossroads, I do not ask that you hunt dragons with me. That road is finished, is done. Two others open before us, and it is upon their trails that we make our way.

"On the first path, we have the choice to disperse, to relinquish our bonds with no sacrifice of honor. If this is what you desire, I wish you well on your way."

Frowns of confusion returned to her ranks. But she would not leave them hopeless in the face of so much loss and sacrifice.

Desdemona raised her hands by her side, in the open gesture Ellis had always used to speak to their assemblies.

"However, if you would stand with me, I swear to you that we shall make such an end as we have envisioned. The transformation of Draykemire may not come to pass while breath still flows through our lungs, but so long as we fight and we win others to our cause, we will eventually see our people freed. We will see the Draykemire we have bled for, that our friends died for, come to be."

At this, her solders cheered. They clasped one another around the shoulders and kissed each other on the cheek.

The task before them wasn't easy. They would need a new strategy, one that allowed them to survive beyond this generation, one that protected Draykemire from the in-fighting of her family—a rebellion that planted seeds.

Their fight wasn't about elevating her name above Tavian's. Not anymore. Whoever sat upon Draykemire's throne, the fate of its people would be the same.

She could see it now, the truth from which she'd shielded her eyes.

They strove for a new Draykemire altogether, one where the child of an Orbaskier and a dragon might choose which life they wanted to lead.

CHAPTER NINE
THE DRAGON

You know my story now, and my shame.

I must ask that you leave me in peace, for your safety as much as my own. Tavian's forces draw nearer. They hunt Desdemona and myself—there is no reason for you to die as well.

Ah, you are kind, and I thank you. Perhaps I should have known that rebinding my fate to an Orbaskier's would likewise condemn me to their misfortune, but I could not resist. If all goes as it should and she survives, perhaps you will have the chance to meet her as one of her subjects and grow to understand.

You hear my heavy sighs and yet you reprimand one such as myself? If that is truly how you feel, then get out. I won't warn you again. Who are you to scold me? I see the accusation in your eyes, plain as lightning struck across the sky.

I did my best to slay the firemancer the night of Tavian's attack, the one with red-orange scales around his eye.

It was his presence that alerted me to the danger I pose to Desdemona . . . and to our child.

The firemancer wears the same disguise as myself. Even Desdemona, the great slayer of my dragon kin, would not survive the accusation of union with—affection for—a dragon.

Of course I feared to face her after she had learned the truth of who I was. Would not you be afraid to speak to the one you love after they brandished a sword in your face and sought nothing more than to slay you?

I had hoped in vain that if she could care for me, if she could understand, that she might see a new way forward.

But in this, as in so much else, I placed my trust in the wrong hands.

I act now not for myself or even my love, but for the fate of the child we share. The people of Draykemire are not so understanding as you. They would never allow me or a child of mine to live. Desdemona will have no choice but to keep the secret close. Tavian would despise any heir, even his own, and hers all the more so.

But the child of his enemy and a blood-heir to the throne? I may as well have surrendered Desdemona and the babe to the firemancer myself.

He will track me here, and we shall fight.

Only one dragon will survive.

Ah, once again, you are kind to say so. I too held close in my heart that ours might be a story for the ages.

Wait.

Do you sense that, upon the air?

The firemancer is not coming nearer as I had planned.

He approaches Desdemona instead.

Such is love in the end, is it not? So few of the choices

we make matter, and even then, they depend upon others, outside of our control.

I cannot leave her to defend herself alone. She knows my secret, yes, but she remains unaware of the power of the one who stalks close.

I must away.

Take care of yourself and your order. I hope our story serves you well.

The clouds gather, and lightning will soon strike.

This eve, I will bring a storm the likes of which none in Draykemire have ever witnessed.

And I will rejoin my lover's side before the night is through.

DESDEMONA

Desdemona and her soldiers set out into the wilds of Draykemire once more. But this time, as they sent word to the villages, they sought to bring a new message, one not of the hope of a queen, but of the Draykemire their queen would see their cities become, a Draykemire free of tyranny.

As summer passed and autumn's chill spread, Desdemona settled into her fort in the northwestern mountains, the range where her father, before his brother betrayed him, had once held sway.

Here, she and her soldiers would make their final stand.

Here, she would give birth to her child.

And the new world would have a chance to be.

Tavian's firemancer continued to track them. He burned the villages nearest by.

They would starve to death before the week was out. But the mage didn't intend to see them live even that long.

His forces gathered. Stormclouds rolled in off the sea.

Desdemona was standing upon the ramparts of the fort, her own tiny kingdom, when the first contractions came. They brought with them the rumble of thunder that had accompanied her child's father before he had flown away.

Her knees crumpled beneath her with the second wave. Desdemona caught herself on the stacked stones. Though the sentinel archers sprinted toward her, Isolde was the first by her side.

The soldiers followed Isolde's bidding. They helped Desdemona to the center of the fort as Tavian's forces prepared their attack outside.

"It will be close," she said to Isolde with tears in her eyes. Their friendship had healed over the months of her pregnancy. Most nights they remained side by side. They held space for the two who were absent, for Ellis who waited for his love, and for Sharr'kahn, the dragon who could not, would not be there.

"You will make it in time," Isolde insisted. A faint purple glow caught behind her eyes. "You will witness your son's first breath, I have seen it."

Desdemona nodded and took the seer's hand.

Her soldiers gathered into their formations without her to drive them on.

She had encouraged them instead to leave her to her ill-fortune, but they would not. Instead, her numbers had grown. It was not for her that they gathered, but for the dream they shared.

The dream Tavian would see crushed before it could grow.

But as every autumn bulb, patiently waiting for spring, the roots had already begun their journey underground.

Isolde coaxed Desdemona through the rigors of birth. Several farmhands had joined their number. They aided with bundles of cloth and boiled water and followed Isolde's precise instructions for the various tinctures she had prepared.

"It's time," the seer pronounced.

The farmhands brought Desdemona up into a crouch over the bedroll and piled cloth. They supported her elbows.

Desdemona threw her head back as the contractions roiled and strengthened like the waves of the sea beyond the fort walls. There hadn't been time to repair the thatch in the roof before the soldiers cut off their escape routes and burned any reeds they might have used.

The tendons of her neck tensed as she cried out. As Isolde exclaimed that the baby was emerging.

And a dragon flew low overhead.

His scales were golden, lightning hardened into armored bark. Antlers arched off the top of his head and caught the storm clouds in their reach.

Desdemona sobbed at the sight of him, half joy, half disbelief.

He couldn't be here. Once the fighting began, not even a dragon would be able to break his way free.

But he had come to her aid nonetheless.

And with his arrival, he offered their son a chance.

Sharr'kahn flew in arching circles across the sky. He breathed out crackles of lightning around the base of the camp.

Her soldiers shouted, their cries matching her own.

They couldn't know. About this, Isolde had been certain. The secret would remain theirs and theirs alone.

One of her scouts ran breathless into the room. The dragon's breath had covered the outside of their fort in thick brambles that Tavian's men would have to skin themselves alive to break through.

Sharr'kahn had carved out the time their son would need.

With a final push and cry, Isolde pulled Desdemona's son into her arms.

The baby screamed with new life. Desdemona lowered down onto her knees and rolled onto her side. "Bring him to me," she croaked to Isolde.

The seer did as she bid. Her eyes brimmed with tears.

Desdemona wiped her blood from her son's head with the hem of her shirt. "Your father's wall will not hold them back forever," she murmured. "One way or another, they'll find a way through." She pressed a kiss to the forehead covered over with dark hair, like hers, and imparted her blessing. *May you have your father's eyes, and Ellis's gift with the sword, little one. And may you find one like Isolde to guide you, and remain always by your side.*

"Isolde."

The seer had stepped back. Her handmaiden's lips trembled. She tried to avoid Desdemona's gaze.

Desdemona called to her again.

This time Isolde obeyed. She knelt at Desdemona's side.

"I issue to you my final command."

"No, my lady, please—"

Desdemona swallowed down the knot in her throat. "Take my son from my arms and my stallion from the stables. There is a village less than a few hectares away, beyond the ones they burned."

She knew these mountains better than any of Tavian's scouts. This one would have been too small, beneath his firemancer's notice. There, her son would have a chance at new life.

Tears fell onto the earthen floor from Isolde's cheeks. Her shoulders shook, but her cries made no sound.

Her son suckled greedily at her breast, the only time they would be together in this way.

"Take him there, and watch over him as best you can. Find someone to raise him as their own." She instructed Isolde to take the remaining gold from her pouch and gift it to the family. The coins were hardly fitting for the employment of a knight, much less an Orbaskier heir.

"Jekk," she called her son by name, the first and only time, "my little warrior. The time will come when you will live by the sword, but I place this boon of hope over you— that one day, the wandering of your feet and careful tending of your blade will bring you into arms that love you. May you ride into your destiny with love close by your side."

Her tears bathed her son's head, but she persevered through this last. If her ancestors were set upon condemning her, at least her son would be free of their vow. "Those who came before us would have this land be yours, but I wish for you something more. Holding the throne alone means nothing. If you would serve Draykemire, attend the good of its people instead. Topple the throne your ancestors would see you rule. And carve out a path all your own."

She cried again as she placed her son in Isolde's arms. "Ride well my friend. May the winds be on your side."

Isolde rose, Jekk a tiny bundle in her arms.

Desdemona caught one last sight of her son as the seer slipped beyond the door.

Her best warriors fell in behind. They would ride out with the seer and ensure her exit from the camp.

They would give their lives in service to her, as too many had before them.

Desdemona buried her head in the pillows gathered at the top of her bedroll. The farmhands drifted away from her side.

A salty sea breeze fluttered in to embrace her, rippling off the rage of the sea.

Sharr'kahn's storm still crackled overhead.

The clouds above shifted. Thick smoke rose in pillars, and a distant shout reached her ears.

The firemancer had broken through the dragon's defenses.

Soon, they would find their way inside.

Desdemona dragged herself to her feet and clasped her sword tight. She donned her armor for one final battle. As the smoke gathered, and petals of ash rained down, she emerged from the inner rooms of the fort to the open skies of the courtyard.

The dragon bellowed as he laid eyes upon her.

And her lover flew down.

They made a strange and fearsome pair, these two who fought back wave upon wave of Tavian's forces.

The onslaught was unrelenting. A poisoned arrow struck through Desdemona's chest. And a powerful warrior's blade cleaved her side before she sheered her sword across his chest.

The firemancer hovered ever in the distance. His black

robes and white hair glimmered through the heat of the surrounding flames.

Desdemona groaned as a second arrow struck her. She collapsed against Sharr'kahn's hide.

Her dragon lover bellowed, scaled nose upraised to storm clouds above. He coiled tight around her, shielded her.

Her soldiers gave a final push at driving their rivals away.

Their sacrifice carved through the will of fate and spared a moment for the lovers.

And then Tavian's will returned to hold sway.

But in that moment, Sharr'kahn held Desdemona close. *"It was my dearest wish to save you, my love,"* he sighed into her mind.

Desdemona placed her forehead against the glimmering bark of her lover's scales. His head was as tall as she. She sobbed and hugged him tighter. "And mine was to be by your side."

She whispered to him of their son, born with his father's storm-tossed eyes.

Sharr'kahn's growl rumbled low in his throat. He lifted his claw and placed a single talon beneath her chin. Desdemona wrapped her arm around the talon and leaned into his touch. She closed her eyes and found herself returned to the nights they spent together, her lover staring into her eyes.

This would have been enough, in the end, had their lives not entailed that they would be set against one another from the start.

He had seen past the wrongs of her family line, had seen through her fear and hatred for what they might share. Desdemona bit her lips together and opened her eyes. "You are all I wanted from this life," Desdemona rasped around the smoke and bile that clung to her throat. "And loving you has finally made it worth the living."

Sharr'kahn's whisper rustled in answer, the thunder she had waited for every night for the months they'd been apart. *"I will find you upon the tree of silver,"* he promised.

Desdemona clutched the words close to her heart. She had dismissed the magic of being near him as a reflection of her feelings, nothing more. But instead, she found a deep well of magic that rippled out from his being and settled high among the clouds, a well that each dragon possessed, unique to this world.

The dying queen relaxed, and Sharr'kahn guided her body to the ground.

"Wait for me there, my love," he said over Desdemona as darkness pooled. *"I will join you soon."*

Sharr'kahn's storms made the promise real. His love for Desdemona, and hers for him, sent a ripple through the threads of fate. Their souls met upon the boughs of their ancestors' tree, forever bound together.

EPILOGUE

The town criers of Draykemire shouted from the rooftops that the last dragon was dead. In one fell swoop, the king routed the usurper to the throne and rid the lands of her and the foul beast she'd sworn into her service. Thanks to the king's bravery and his cunning acts, the land might once again be returned to the darkness they had for centuries known.

Tavian's soldiers kept secret the fierce fight they faced at the dragon's side, he who protected the body of the usurper from their grasp. The dragon sealed her away in a tomb of glimmering brambles. The vines' shimmering bark matched his scales.

The king ordered the dragon's bones dragged back to the seat of his power in the growing city of Sanctuary. His most loyal firemancer oversaw the task. They burned away the dragon's scales over the course of months until finally the bones were bare. The mages arranged them behind Tavian's throne so that the dragon's magic would cloak and cover their king for always, prolonging his rule.

Desdemona's soldiers cut out their tongues before they

revealed the truth of their lady's state the night of the battle. They refused to confide, even under torment, what had happened to the seer who had been a constant by her side.

The king's spies hunted and killed any who whispered of a second uprising, those who threatened Tavian with the promise that another Orbaskier yet lived.

But on the edge of the kingdom, within the confines of a small village, the king's fated enemy grew.

On the stormiest night in Draykemire, a dark-haired sorceress with a babe in arms knocked on the door of two pig farmers. "Fifteen gold to take the child and raise him as your own," she said. The sorceress held out the bag first and then the babe. She knew well enough the ways of hungry peasants.

"Are you his mother?" the woman asked. She reached out with pity toward the sorceress.

"I am not. My lady is. Finding care for the child was her dying wish."

The farmer gasped when he saw the blood-soaked blanket that covered the child. "The baby—"

"The blood is mine," the sorceress said. She pressed a hand to cover the arrow wounds in her abdomen. A sword had slashed her side.

"We will raise him as our own," the farmer said. He wrapped an arm around his wife and their new child.

The sorceress bowed her head in thanks, though those receiving her gesture had no idea of its significance for one of her rank. Her eyes glowed bright as jade, and she spoke her benediction over the child. "Fortune favor you, Jekk

Stormborn," the sorceress said, the same blessing her mother had uttered over the lady her daughter would serve at Desdemona's birth.

She drifted away into the night and lost herself in the storm.

The woods embraced her as one of their own.

As she had foreseen several months before, this was not the end of her tale. She lingered on in the woods and watched as the baby grew into a child and then a man.

His fate changed when another gale blew through the small town of his childhood. Many of the villagers did not survive, but he did.

Until that fateful day, when she joined her own love in Astralei, the sorceress watched her lady's child from afar with a careful eye. For years, his mother's ferocity kept him alive. But something else propelled him on, something beyond determination.

He had the same searching spirit as his father before him. The same persistent sense of hope.

Stormborn indeed.

WORLDS OF HEROES AND HEIRS AWAIT!

I hope you loved this standalone novella for the future *Tree of Silver* epic fantasy saga! I had so much fun weaving Desdemona and Sharr'kahn's tale, and I cannot wait to share their son Jekk's journey with you in the years to come! (He *does* make an appearance outside his future series in *Shadows Beneath*, *Age of Azuria* book five!)

If you'd like to see the future of Draykemire several hundred years after the events of *Stormborn*, I invite you into a similarly spellbinding tale, this one also starring an heir and involving a curse, but instead of a dragon, her counterpart is a nobleman by day and assassin by night...

Little does he know that *she* is also in disguise, and beneath her courtesan's role within his rival's house, secrets that might forever change their world are waiting to be unraveled.

Explore Draykemire's future in the *Heir of Lilith* epic romantic fantasy series!

THE COURTLY INTRIGUE OF DRAYKEMIRE ISN'T THE END OF THE STORY...

The world of Eldura continues to expand, particularly in the growth of its magics and its technologies. Hundreds more years pass between Silas and Natalya's adventure in *Phantom* and the events that unfold near the turning of an era.

Events starring a phoenix and a warrior wielding flame shape an era that resonates throughout history. An era that will come to be known as the War of the Champions.

A rebellious druid, a disillusioned warrior, and the chance to save their world from destruction—a dark and epic adventure awaits in *Phoenix Rising*!

IF YOU'RE LOOKING FOR MORE INTRIGUE AND ADVENTURE

Then look no further than *Buried Heroes* and the *Age of Azuria* epic fantasy series!

The walls of Linolynn's court are closing in around

half-elf Iellieth Amastacia. She can no longer escape the forced marriage her stepfather has arranged for her.

But on the day she's to depart for the cruel northern kingdom, fate intervenes. The amulet she inherited from the elven father she's never met whisks her away to a frigid mountainside. Trapped within is a hero of Eldura who now finds himself within an entirely new world, Azuria. And his soul is bound to the half-elf who awakened him.

Buried Heroes is an epic fantasy adventure filled with unforgettable characters, druidic magic, and immersive worldbuilding with a slow burn romance subplot. Follow Iellieth on her adventure though ancient forests as she discovers the ancient relics—and hidden heroes—destined to save her world.

JOURNEY DEEPER INTO ELDURA

For character art reveals, fantasy map deep-dives, and all the latest happenings in Eldura, visit bethballbooks.com/join to be part of my newsletter community, the Circle of Story.

For author-signed print books, exclusive character art, and upcoming special editions, visit bethballbooks.shop.

ACKNOWLEDGMENTS

My love and thanks to Jonathan, who has loved and believed in this novella from the beginning and whose character in our duet ttRPG game inspired Jekk. The storyverse we've made together is always expanding, which fills me with endless delight.

Second, an outpouring of gratitude to my editor, Kristen. Thank you for your words of encouragement. Working with you on *Stormborn* was so much fun!

And finally, to you, dear reader: I hope you enjoyed *Stormborn* as much as I have enjoyed sharing it with you! There will be a full series in the future, *Tree of Silver*, that picks up with Jekk's adventures.

ABOUT THE AUTHOR

Beth Ball is a weaver of words and worlds spinning stories of druidic magic and the power of nature that span the epic fantasy realms of Eldura and Azuria. If you enjoy lyrical tales of action and adventure, dragons, werewolves, fae, wily foxes, and more, then grab your enchanted amulet, flaming longsword, poisoned dagger, or other mystical accessory of choice, and let's start our adventure! You can find more of Beth's work and the legends of Eldura at bethballbooks.shop.

GLOSSARY

The following glossary entries may contain light spoilers for the worldbuilding and characters of Stormborn. For a more comprehensive list alongside lore and cross-series interconnections, visit bethballbooks.com/glossary.

WORLDS & PLANES

Planes of Life, *three interconnected planes,* Eldura, Shadowlands, and Brightlands
Elemental Planes, one for each element, ruled over by and encompassing the power of each elemental titan
Astralei, spirit plane
Eldura, central world of the planes of life, made up of kingdoms and great cities including the kingdom of Draykemire

Kingdoms

Draykemire, kingdom ruled by Tavian; once ruled by

dragons until they were overthrown by the Orbaskier
family line
Verrain, neighboring kingdom nearest to Draykemire
through the portals between Eldura and the Shadowlands
Neverune, older name for the region that now holds
Draykemire, Respite, and Vestige

Court of Draykemire

King Tavian Orbaskier, ruler of Draykemire
Desdemona Orbaskier, would-be queen of Draykemire

ELEMENTAL TITANS

Gaia, titan of earth
Ignis, titan of fire
Atamos, titan of air
Ilona, titan of light
Thalyssa, titan of water
Nyx, titan of darkness
Verdigris, titan of nature, *destroyed and transformed into the
three planes of life*
Izadra, titan of space, *destroyed and transformed into the
spirit plane, Astralei*

DEITIES

Alessandra, "the dark goddess"
Cassandra, goddess of fate
Rasvana, creator goddess of dragons
Ruka, betrayer god who serves alongside Alessandra

LOREKEEPERS' ARCHIVE

From the lorekeepers' archive, the legend of the ancient kingdom of Neverune and how Gaia divided it into three.

NEVERUNE, THE DIVIDED KINGDOM

Legend tells that before Ruka's betrayal sent the city of Orison into the depths of the sea, there was a great and ancient kingdom, Neverune, ruled through the ages by wisdom and might by a sacred line of kings. The kingdom withstood the insistent attacks of Alessandra—the dark goddess was envious of the kingdom's prosperity and longed to overtake the throne for herself. But the line of kings persisted in protecting their city. And their rule lasted for one thousand years.

But like all such stories, such a faery tale could not continue forever.

What the line of kings did not know, in spite of their wisdom and the careful governance of their seers, was that calamity waited with carefully folded wings. And it chose the perfect moment to strike.

One thousand years after Alessandra's betrayal of the elemental titans, they who carefully governed the workings of the prime plane of Eldura, another mortal rose to the power of godhood.

The champion of water, right-hand of Thalyssa, betrayed the city he had been appointed to protect. The earth around Orison splintered and burst, sending the city into the gaping maw of the sea. With the sacrifice of thousands of souls, the former champion, Ruka, rose to Alessandra's side.

A god of trickery, lies, and deceit, Ruka twisted the minds of Neverune's great kings and turned them against the people they had been appointed to serve. A new line of leaders rose up in their stead, determined to be protectors of the people and to rid the land of the kings' corruption.

War and infighting tore apart the ancient kingdom. Thousands more lives were lost.

Distressed by what transpired in their realms, the titans intervened. Thalyssa sent the waters to divide the kingdom, to shrink the influence and power of any single king. Gaia called mountains to rise up from the earth and divide the kingdom still further.

It was not the first time the titans had resorted to separation and rising waters to quell rebellion and bloodshed upon the planes of life, nor would it be the last. From their workings, eventually, peace returned. The city of Respite grew up from the western mountains. To the north, the people created Vestige, a land ravaged by the fallen line of kings who left much of the city in ruins with their fall. The most powerful of the three arose in the east. There, the new line of kings continued in their rule. And at the heart of the throne of Draykemire, the dream remains: that one day, the three cities might be united again. This is the true promise of the kings' rule.

❧

Also from the lorekeepers' archive, the origin story of the dragons of Eldura.

THE LEGEND OF RASVANA AND THE CREATION OF THE DRAGONS

Long before the First Age and the separation of the planes that followed their creation, the goddess Rasvana looked with envy upon the first creatures of the wolf-god Fenrir—the daimon—wild wolves who traversed the planes of the world, melding leaf, limb, and flower with their fur and living in communion with their creator deity.

Rasvana saw the adoration the daimon bore their creator, and she wished the same adulations for herself. Other deities discouraged her, saying she underestimated the weight of so many dependents, that she should maintain her freedom. But Rasvana was not a goddess to take others' advice.

"Make me a people," she bade the wolf-god. "Give them wings and scales and a living breath. Grant them eyes sharp as daggers and infinite souls in near-infinite bodies. Make them as invincible as I am."

"You are a goddess in your own right," Fenrir replied. "Cast such a people yourself."

Rasvana gnashed her teeth and withdrew to the deepest forests of the world. There she tried, but the creatures who emerged fell short of her visions of what those made to look like herself should be. From these first trials, the drakes, wyverns, and winged serpents emerged, but the goddess wanted something more.

She returned to Fenrir's side. "My efforts have failed. You know already how to craft a people. The daimon look to you to lead them. Teach me your method that I may have the same."

"We must each find our path on our own," the wolf-god answered. "I cannot aid you and preserve my energy for my second people." In this he spoke of the Lycan who were as yet little more than a bright spark in the corner of the wolf-god's eyes.

Curls of smoke slithered from the goddess's nostrils. She trailed a taloned claw around her sister goddess Cassandra's shoulders and tugged her closer. "Let the goddess of fate bear witness to a pact between you and I, then, Fenrir. As you are so confident and wise, you will not mind playing against me in a game of chance. Should you win, you and your wolves will go on as you are. But should you lose, you will serve me a year and a day and teach me to craft a people of my own, those who will fear and adore me in turn."

Fenrir grew tired of the goddess's demands, but he saw the golden glint in her eyes. Rasvana would not allow the matter to rest until she was satisfied. His people would survive his year of captivity, he knew, but the goddess would not count herself so lucky after trying to bridle a wolf, even for so short a time. "Very well, I accept your challenge." The wolf-god bowed his head to Cassandra whose eyes widened, but the goddess of fate held her counsel.

Thrice the deities competed in a game of chance of

Cassandra's design. In the first, Fenrir took the match. The second fell to Rasvana. The goddess licked her lips along her jagged rows of teeth for their third match. Fenrir shut his eyes and breathed his prayer into Cassandra's mind.

With a gasp from the goddesses, the pieces fell in Rasvana's favor. Her delight was so great that billows of flame rippled forth from her mouth and rent apart the clouds in the sky. "Victory is mine," she cried.

The daimon howled in despair, believing their lord to have been taken from them against his will. For a year and a day, they stalked the lands, searching for Rasvana's hiding place.

And for a year and a day, Fenrir wove his revenge. He taught the goddess to pour her power into her people, showed her how to weave the fabric of her being into scales and skin. Yet he withheld his own dearly won knowledge of the nature of creation—were the creatures Rasvana designed to be as powerful as the goddess wished, they would each require a spark of godhood itself.

Fenrir taught the goddess to grant each of her creations a gift, divine magic in the form of a changent scale. These would allow them to survive among the fae and later the Lycan for they could hide the secret of their heritage in a changing form. These scales granted them each a unique magical expression—breath that could command shadows, a wind so powerful as to fell even ancient trees. Rasvana poured out her memories, her longing, her greed, making each of her creations more wonderful than the last.

Cassandra watched in silence, held by the pact she and Fenrir had made that day of Rasvana's bargain—*Do not interfere*, the wolf-god had commanded. *Your sister's reckless-ness yields a price to be paid.*

He was not wrong, the maker of the Lycan. Cassandra knew this in her heart. *I ask but one thing in return*, she answered. *When your lesson is through, entrust my sister's children to me, that I may watch over her soul, the work of her life, until even the worlds yet to come are no more.*

Fenrir knew better than to argue with the goddess of fate—such is the blessing and curse of Cassandra's magic after all. *Let it be as you say.* And the matter was done.

The goddess of fate drew nearer as the days of Fenrir's captivity came to a close. "Is it always so tiring to create?" Cassandra overheard her sister say to Fenrir. The plumes of smoke that had once graced her nostrils were little more than a soft spring breeze.

"Not always," the wolf-god answered, "but in the case of your children, they will be mightier than any other groups of beings could possibly be."

"That is good," Rasvana sighed. "I wish them strength, longevity, and cleverness above all."

The goddess's eyes fluttered shut as she wove the last changent scale into being. Her form rippled and faded into little more than mist and voice.

"What will you call them, my lady?" the wolf-god asked Rasvana's fading form.

"Dragons," she answered, the fire of her gaze finding Fenrir as the last pieces of her essence flitted into the changent scale. "Our battle is not over, Fenrir. For you have tricked me once, but my thousand children will live on through the ages and seek to fool you again and again."

"I would expect nothing less," Fenrir said with a smile. He planted a kiss upon the remnants of Rasvana's brow. "You have done what no other deity had the heart to do," he said in benediction, "and your children will live on, the mightiest in all of creation—"

"Until the very ends of all the world," Cassandra added.

The pair turned from the changent scales and the sleeping, glimmering eggs left in Rasvana's wake. Cassandra smiled sadly as she perceived the lowered head of the wolf-god, the slow thump of his heart as he returned to the daimon, his first people. Such is the love that will make and unmake the worlds again and again, Cassandra thought to herself.

That year and a day left Fenrir forever changed. He has longed for the challenge and presence of the great dragon mother ever since. Neither his daimon nor the Lycan can fill the hole in his heart that she left, for in the final dragon, to protect and seal Rasvana's creation, Fenrir left a part of himself.

And for Rasvana, she who poured her divine essence into each of her thousand offspring who would be born and die across all the ages of the world, she lives on in dwindling number, but her divinity beats still, sparkling in changent scales, each as unique and magical as the goddess who created them.